Dora's Thanksgiving

by Sarah Willson
illustrated by Robert Roper

SCHOLASTIC INC.

New York   Toronto   London   Auckland   Sydney
Mexico City   New Delhi   Hong Kong   Buenos Aires

¡Hola! I'm Dora. Today is Thanksgiving. We are going to have a big meal with my family and friends.

Do you know who I am most thankful for? They are two people in my family, and they take care of me every day. Who are they?

I am most thankful for my *mami* and *papi*.
Today I am helping them get ready for our
Thanksgiving dinner. I helped my *mami* bake these pies.

There is another person in my family who I am thankful for. She is older and she tells me stories about my *mami* when she was a little girl.

It's *mi abuela*! *Abuela* teaches me about all sorts of things. I love her a lot!

We are having Thanksgiving dinner at *Abuela's* house today. I get to carry the pies!

Do *you* have someone special in your family that you are thankful for? Who is it?

I have a very good friend that I am thankful for. He likes to go on adventures with me. He lives in a tree house and has a long tail. Do you know who it is?

It's my friend Boots. Come on, Boots.
You can help me carry these pies to
Abuela's house.

I have another friend that I'm thankful for. I carry her everywhere. Anything I need, she has inside for me. In Spanish, I call her *Mochila*. Do you know who it is?

It's Backpack! She can speak Spanish and English, just like me.

I have a friend who always helps me find my way. He lives inside Backpack's pocket. Do you know who it is?

It's Map! I am thankful for Map. Anywhere I need to go, Map helps me get there.

Do *you* have a friend that you are thankful for? Who is *your* friend?

Wait. I think I hear Swiper the fox. He will try to swipe our pies! Do you see Swiper? If you see him, you have to say "Swiper, no swiping!"

We did it!
That Swiper is always trying to swipe our stuff. I am really thankful that we stopped Swiper!

Look! All my friends and family are here.
It's almost time for Thanksgiving dinner!

Before we begin eating our Thanksgiving meal everyone talks about what they are thankful for. I am thankful for so many things: my family and friends, and the sun and the moon, and flowers and adventures, and . . .

Oh! I just thought of one more friend who I am very, very thankful for. I'll give you a hint: This person always helps me. This person comes on adventures with me. And this person is looking at this book right now. Do you know who it is?

It's YOU!
Gracias for being my friend.
Happy Thanksgiving!